Text copyright © 1998 Fox Busters Ltd
Illustrations copyright © 1998 Frank Rodgers

First published in Great Britain in 1998 by
Macdonald Young Books
an imprint of Wayland Publishers Ltd
61 Western Road
Hove
East Sussex
BN3 1JD

Printed and bound in Belgium by Proost International Book Co.

British Library Cataloguing in Publication Data available.

ISBN: 0 7500 2568 9

# Dick King-Smith

# MRS JOLLY'S BROLLY

## Illustrated by Frank Rodgers

MACDONALD YOUNG BOOKS

Mrs Jolly was a witch.
Mind you, she didn't look like one.

Witches are skinny and wrinkled.
Mrs Jolly was plump and
apple-cheeked.

Witches have long lank black hair and
hooked noses and pointed chins.

Mrs Jolly had short curly grey hair and
a snub nose and two nice little fat chins.

Witches always scowl.
Mrs Jolly always smiled.

Finally, witches have black cats,
and Mrs Jolly's cat was a ginger one.

One day they were sitting together by the fire when the ginger cat said, "Isn't it the Witches' Annual Reunion Party next week?" "Oh yes, you're right, but I don't know how I'm going to get there. I haven't been on a broomstick for years, it's so uncomfy," said Mrs Jolly.

"No problem," said the cat and he strolled over to a corner of
the room where Mrs Jolly had propped her umbrella.
It was one of those large brightly coloured umbrellas, blue
and red and green and yellow.
"You could use this," said the ginger cat, "like a hot-air balloon.
Just open it up, hang on to the handle and put a spell on it."
Mrs Jolly giggled.

"I could, couldn't I?" she said, and she went out on to the lawn, opened up the big, coloured umbrella, held it above her head and said,

"You're a lovely magic brolly,
With your colours bright and jolly,
I'll hold your handle nice and tight,
And then we'll try a maiden flight."

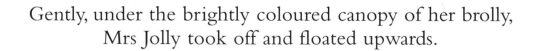

Gently, under the brightly coloured canopy of her brolly,
Mrs Jolly took off and floated upwards.

The cat watched as she drifted up to tree-top height and then
he called, "How about getting down again?"
"Easy!" cried Mrs Jolly, and to the umbrella she said,

> "You're a lovely magic brolly,
> With your colours bright and jolly,
> So bring me downwards, nice and neat,
> And land me lightly on my feet."

"That looked fun," said the cat
as Mrs Jolly touched down on the grass.
"It was!" she said. "I'll use it to go to the witches' party."

Mrs Jolly quite enjoyed the party, even though many of the other witches gave her dirty looks. A broomstick, they considered, was the only proper form of transport for a witch, but here was this one dropping in under a striped umbrella, if you please!

Back home again, Mrs Jolly said to her cat, "That was
tiring, I must say, having to hang on to the handle of the brolly.
If only I had somewhere to sit," and she sat down on one of the
kitchen chairs.
"No problem," said the cat. "All you have to do is hook the
handle of the brolly through the back of that chair."

"I could, couldn't I?' said Mrs Jolly, and she carried the chair
out on to the lawn, opened the brolly, hooked its handle
through and said,

"You're a lovely magic brolly,
With your colours bright and jolly,
I've hooked your handle on my chair,
Now lift me upwards in the air,"

and up they went. Mrs Jolly
sitting comfortably on her
chair and waving to the
ginger cat below, as the
brolly rose higher.
And higher. And higher.

Till at last the cat lost sight of Mrs Jolly and her brolly,
so high had they risen.
"Oh dear," he said. "What's gone wrong?"
In fact nothing had gone wrong at all. Mrs Jolly was simply
enjoying herself.
At first she could look down to see her house, and then
all the streets round her house. Then she spotted a big notice
advertising a Great Hot-air Balloon Race.

"I like races," said Mrs Jolly to herself. "It'd be rather fun to go in for this one. Who knows, I might win."

Higher and higher she rose now, looking down on first the whole town and then the whole county, until at last she could see the whole of the country, with the blue sea at the edges.

Then Mrs Jolly looked at her watch.

"Goodness me!" she said. "It's not only me that flies, time's flying too," and to the brolly she said,

"Now then, lovely magic brolly,
With your colours bright and jolly,
We must descend immediately,
Or else I shall be late for tea."

"Thought I'd lost you," said the ginger cat when Mrs Jolly
landed on the lawn again.
"Sorry," said Mrs Jolly. "I got carried away."

Now, so as to keep her magic brolly a secret,
Mrs Jolly mostly flew at night (which
witches are good at doing).

Sometimes even when it was raining because
the brolly kept her dry (which umbrellas
are good at doing).

But on the day of the Great Hot-air Balloon Race, she couldn't resist going along.
"I'll just watch the start of the race," she said to the ginger cat.
"I see," he said. "It's a beautiful day, why are you taking your brolly?"
"Oh, to keep the sun off," she replied.

The ginger cat put a paw up in front of his face, to hide a gingery grin.

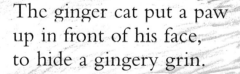

There were hundreds of hot-air balloons lined up in a great field: ordinary-shaped ones with all kinds of different names written on them, and some shaped like bottles or castles, and one like a teddy bear.

And there were thousands of people who had come to watch the start of the race.

There was so much noise and excitement as all the different balloons lifted off into the sky, that no one noticed a plump little old lady with short curly grey hair and a snub nose and two nice fat little chins, sitting on a kitchen chair in a far corner of the great field, holding above her head a brightly coloured umbrella.

Mrs Jolly waited till all the balloons were out of sight and all the people had gone home and then she hooked the handle of her brolly through the back of the kitchen chair and said,

"OK, lovely magic brolly,
With your colours bright and jolly,
Now lift me up and take me high,
Into the sunny summery sky.
And follow at your fastest pace,
For we are going to win this race!"

You can guess the rest I expect.
Once high enough, Mrs Jolly's
brolly tore along in pursuit of all
the other hot-air balloons with
Mrs Jolly swinging wildly
underneath it on her
kitchen chair.

Soon it caught up with the slowest balloon (the one shaped like a teddy bear, it was) and so surprised were the people in its basket to see her that one of them overbalanced and would have fallen out if someone hadn't grabbed his legs.

It was the same with the other balloonists. None of them could believe their eyes as the witch sailed past them, waving gaily and shouting, "Snails!" or "Tortoises!" or "Slowcoaches!"
So shocked were they that some turned on their hot-air burners for too long and so rose up much too high, and some forgot to turn theirs on at all and sank to the ground.

In a very short time Mrs Jolly had passed the leaders, and indeed she arrived at the finish so long before anyone was expected that there was no one there to see, and no one to hear her say,

"Well done, lovely magic brolly,
With your colours bright and jolly!
Wasn't that a bit of fun!
Hip, hip, hip, hooray, we've won!
We're the best, no doubt of that!
Let's go home and tell the cat."

It was a funny thing, but the crew of the first balloon to finish never said that they had seen anything strange. They didn't want it known that they had been beaten by an old lady sitting on a kitchen chair under a striped umbrella.

Nor did the crew of the second balloon to finish or the third or any of the others.

So no one knew that the
Great Hot-air Balloon Race was won
by Mrs Jolly's brolly.
Till now.

But you believe it, I'm sure.
The ginger cat certainly did when she told him.
He grinned his gingery grin, and as for Mrs Jolly,
well, she just smiled her jolly smile.

If you have enjoyed this book, why not try some other terrific picture books published by Macdonald Young Books?

### The Jolly Witch
*Written by Dick King-Smith • Illustrated by Frank Rodgers*
Mrs Jolly is a school caretaker by day and a witch by night! She uses her magic powers to help her clean the school – until one special night when she casts a rather unusual spell on the vacuum cleaner…
ISBN: 0 7500 0203 4 (Also available as a Big Book)

### Mrs Jollipop
*Written by Dick King-Smith • Illustrated by Frank Rodgers*
Mrs Jolly, the lovable witch, is now a lollipop lady, which is why the children all call her Mrs Jollipop. But Mrs Jolly just can't resist using her magic powers. Her lollipop doesn't always say STOP CHILDREN and her feet don't always remain safely on the ground!
ISBN: 0 7500 2017 2

### The Huge Bag of Worries
*Written by Virginia Ironside • Illustrated by Frank Rodgers*
Wherever Jenny goes, her worries follow her – in a big blue bag! They are there when she goes swimming, when she is watching TV, and even when she is in the lavatory. Jenny decides they will have to go. But who will help her?
ISBN: 0 7500 2124 1 (Also available as a Big Book)

### Mac and the Big Feet
*Written and illustrated by Frank Rodgers*
Mac is looking forward to having a holiday in the city with his country cousins – there will be so much to see and do! But wherever they go and whatever they do, Mac and his cousins are surrounded by big animals and their big feet. Doesn't anyone realise that little animals are important too?
ISBN 0 7500 2540 9 (h/b) ISBN 0 7500 2541 7 (p/b)

You can buy all these books from your local bookshop, or they can be ordered direct from the publishers. For more information about picture books, write to: *The Sales Department, Macdonald Young Books, 61 Western Road, Hove, East Sussex, BN3 1JD.*